# Disney's TaleSpin
# HER CHANCE TO DREAM

Adapted by
**Naomi McMillan**

Illustrated by
**Vaccaro Associates, Inc.**

MALLARD
PRESS

Twin Books

It was late afternoon at Higher for Hire, and Rebecca was taking phone calls. Each caller had the same question: Where's my cargo?

"I'm afraid it's not here yet," Rebecca said into the phone. "The plane is late." The phone rang again. "I'm sorry, we're running a little late," Rebecca apologized. Then she hung up, ready to explode.

"Baloo! Where are you?" she yelled. *If he is where I think he is*, thought Rebecca, *he's gonna wish he weren't!* She picked up the phone. "Operator? Get me Louie's Place!"

At that moment, Baloo was at Louie's dancing the conga with a hopping lady hippo. Her weight made the floor boards creak and moan and, just as she danced away to a new partner, Baloo and Louie crashed through the floor to a basement Louie didn't even know he had.

It looked exactly like a ship's corridor, complete with a captain's cabin at one end.

"Looky here," said Baloo, pulling a sword from a trunk in the captain's room.

"And dig these cra-azy threads," Louie said, putting on the captain's hat, coat, and boots.

The cabin lanterns began to sway and creak. Ribbons
of light rose from the trunk, snatching the clothes and
sword from Louie and Baloo. Then the objects gathered
in the center of the room, hanging in midair.

"Let's get outta here!" cried Baloo. He and Louie climbed out of the basement and headed for the door, the clothes and sword chasing them. The rest of Louie's customers were not far behind.

Baloo and Louie jumped into the *Sea Duck* and took off.

Back at Higher for Hire, Rebecca tapped her foot impatiently. "I can't wait to hear the dumb excuse Baloo has for being late *this* time!" she said. Then she heard the *Sea Duck* land.

Baloo and Louie raced into the building, then slammed and bolted the door, panting.

"*Well?*" asked Rebecca.

"G-g-ghost!" stuttered Baloo, gesturing toward the restaurant. "At Louie's!"

"Oh, please!" exploded Rebecca, sure that Baloo was making up one of his stories. "Just unload the cargo!"

"Cargo?" said Baloo. "Uhh, I sorta left the cargo at Louie's."

"Then go back and get it," suggested Rebecca through clenched teeth.

"Back there? No way!" said Baloo. "That place
is haunted!"

"We'll see about that," said Rebecca. She dragged
Baloo and Louie to the *Sea Duck*. "We're all going back!"

But when they got to Louie's, all they saw was a great big mess.

"All right, Baloo, let's get the cargo and go back to the office," Rebecca said.

"Who's gonna help me get rid of that kooky spook?" asked Louie. "It scared off my customers."

"If a ghost could close this dump," said Rebecca, "I'd kiss him!" She stormed off.

14

Suddenly Rebecca slipped on a piece of pineapple, sailed across the room and landed on the floor. Just then, a handsome stranger appeared in the doorway.

"Allow me," he said, helping Rebecca up. "Captain Stansbury, at your service."

"Well, now," said Baloo. "Who's that?"

"A gentleman," noted Rebecca, still holding the captain's hand.

"Welcome to Louie's Cafe!" greeted Louie.

"You call this an eating establishment?" said the captain. "Looks to me like you ruined a good sailing ship. If this were my ship I'd . . . I'd . . ."

"Have them flogged?" Rebecca put in, staring deeply
into his eyes.

"Well said, Madam!"

"Take a long walk off a short pier, Becky," Baloo muttered.

Rebecca finally let go of Stansbury's hand, embarrassed. "Well! I've lost all track of time. Come on, Baloo. We have to get going."

"Might I escort you out, my lady?" asked the captain.

"I thought you'd never ask," replied Rebecca.

Louie and Baloo rolled their eyes as Rebecca and the captain left arm in arm.

"I'm gonna nip this in the bud!" said Baloo, reaching the door. But it refused to open. "Becky, come back! Let us out!" he shouted.

Meanwhile, Rebecca was giving the captain a tour of the *Sea Duck*.

"A miracle of engineering!" said Stansbury, as if he'd never seen an airplane. "This ship of the air is yours?" he asked Rebecca, amazed. "Where I'm from, women cook and care for the little ones."

Rebecca thought of her daughter Molly and smiled. "There's that, too," she said.

"I've never met anyone like you," said the captain.

"I was about to say the same thing about you," whispered Rebecca.

In a panic, Louie and Baloo crashed through a wall
of the tavern and landed in the bay. They swam to the
*Sea Duck* as fast as they could and climbed aboard.
When Rebecca saw Baloo, she realized it was time to
get back.

22

"Must you leave?" asked the captain.

"Yes. I left my daughter with the babysitter, and I have to . . ." She stared into the captain's eyes and her words trailed off.

Baloo jumped into the pilot's seat and tried to start the engine. Nothing happened.

"This plane's dead!" muttered Baloo. "We can't get outta here!"

Louie trembled. "It's like someone—or something—wants us to stay."

"Oh, stop it!" snapped Rebecca. "There are no ghosts here. Just you two dummies, me and the cap . . ." But Stansbury had vanished.

By now, it was getting dark and Rebecca was very tired. She announced that she was going to sleep and sent Louie and Baloo back to Louie's to do the same.

"Are we gonna let some spook push us around?" asked Baloo.

"Yeah! I . . . I mean—no!" answered Louie.

"Come on, then," said Baloo. Moments later, he and Louie kicked in the door of the cafe. They put some music on full-blast and marched around banging pots and pans, hoping to scare off the ghost.

Unfortunately, they forgot about the hole in the floor
above the captain's cabin. Louie fell right through it into
the old sea chest, and the lid snapped shut.

Rebecca had been kept awake by all the noise. She grabbed her blanket and trudged up the beach until she found a quiet spot to spend the night.

"Rebecca," someone whispered. Rebecca looked around. "Captain?" she called. She walked in the direction of the voice. Someone bumped into her in the darkness and she gasped.

"Forgive me if I alarmed you," said Stansbury. "I couldn't sleep."

"Nor could I," said Rebecca. Stansbury held out his arm to her and she took it, smiling. The two set off for a walk in the moonlight.

Back at the restaurant, Baloo opened the lid of the trunk in which his friend was trapped. Trembling, Louie held out a diary in one hand, and a painting in the other.

"It's him!" Louie croaked, lifting the portrait of Stansbury for Baloo to see.

"According to this diary," said Louie, "his ship went aground on this very spot—100 years ago! Rebecca doesn't know it, but her captain with the most . . . is a ghost! What are we gonna do, Baloo?"

"We're gonna catch us a ghost!" he said.

Later that night, Stansbury entered Louie's with a sleeping Rebecca in his arms. He laid her on a bench and turned to leave.

"Now!" yelled Baloo, and Stansbury soon found himself caught in a huge net.

"No!" cried Stansbury, reaching toward Rebecca. He quickly drew his sword, slashed the net and stepped free. Then he faced Baloo.

"Skewer me all ya want," dared Baloo. "No ghost is takin' my boss!"

"Rebecca is going with me," insisted Stansbury, lowering his sword.

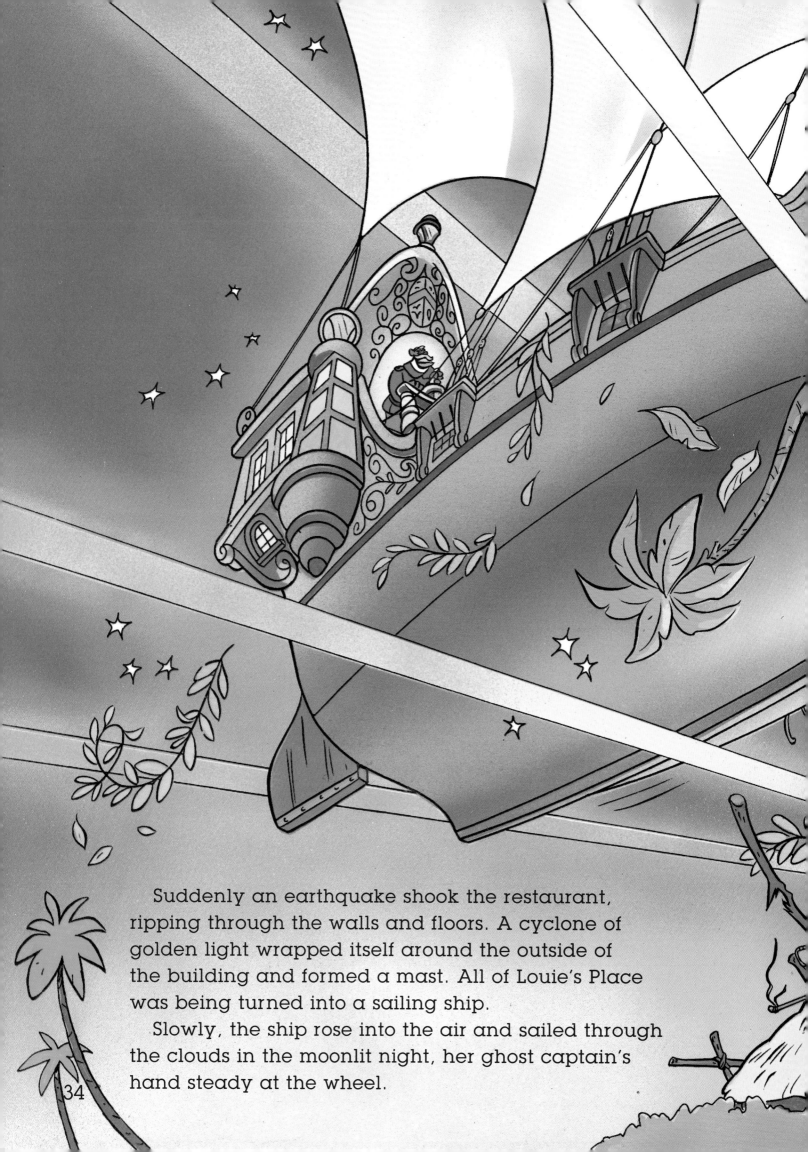

Suddenly an earthquake shook the restaurant,
ripping through the walls and floors. A cyclone of
golden light wrapped itself around the outside of
the building and formed a mast. All of Louie's Place
was being turned into a sailing ship.

Slowly, the ship rose into the air and sailed through
the clouds in the moonlit night, her ghost captain's
hand steady at the wheel.

Rebecca woke up and looked around, smiling. "What a marvelous dream," she said, joining the captain at the wheel of the ship.

The captain smiled, then waved his hand, changing her dress into a flowing gown. Then he grabbed the ship's wheel. "Look, my lady!" he whispered, steering the ship up into a cloud bank. A comet streaked past, and there were stars everywhere.

"Stay with me, Rebecca," said the captain. "The skies are ours to sail for the rest of time."

Louie and Baloo found themselves below deck dressed in navy uniforms, each holding a mop and scrub brush.

They rushed to the top deck, looking for Rebecca. "Time to bust up this party, Becky," said Baloo. "Your captain here is a ghost!"

But the news didn't bother Rebecca. She thought it was all a dream.

Before Baloo could explain that it wasn't, Stansbury snapped his fingers. Once again, Baloo and Louie found themselves on the lower deck.

Louie threw his scrub brush at the wall, but it hit a row of books on a shelf instead. One of them caught his eye. "Oh, baby!" said Louie, reading the title. *Magic Spells of the Sea.*

He leafed through the book and found a spell that would get rid of the mop and brush for good—and another spell that would get rid of Stansbury.

Louie and Baloo went back upstairs to work their magic on the captain.

"Mermaids and herrings and ancient boat slips . . ." Louie began. A golden light surrounded the captain.

"No! Don't!" pleaded Stansbury.

"What're you doing?" cried Rebecca, grabbing the book.

"Gettin' rid of Captain Casanova," explained Louie.

Rebecca ran to the railing, ready to toss the book overboard. "Isn't it enough you guys ruin my life? Must you ruin my dreams, too?"

"Becky, wake up!" said Baloo. "This isn't a dream. It's *real!*"

"Quick, Rebecca," urged Louie. "Finish the spell."

"No! Stay with me," said the captain.

"You've gotta come back with us!" argued Baloo.

"Stop!" cried Rebecca. "I want to stay. I want to be happy!"

Baloo pleaded with her in a gentle voice. "Becky, I want you to be happy, too. But you gotta think of your life. Think of Molly."

"Molly," repeated Rebecca. Slowly, Rebecca came to her senses. She touched Stansbury's cheek. "You've given me a dream forever," said Rebecca. "But my daughter . . . I have to go back."

"I—I understand, Rebecca," said the captain sadly.

As Rebecca finished the spell, the ghost ship rose into the sky.

"I'll wait for you," promised the captain. Then he was gone.

That night, as Rebecca told Molly a bedtime story about a handsome sea captain, she smiled a secret smile. *No matter what happens*, she thought, *I'll always have the dream.*